Emma in Charge

by David McPhail

DUTTON CHILDREN'S BOOKS · NEW YORK

For Kristyn, with love from Papa Dave

DUTTON CHILDREN'S BOOKS
A division of Penguin Young Readers Group

Published by the Penguin Group
Penguin Group (USA) Inc., 375 Hudson Street, New York, New York 10014, U.S.A.
Penguin Group (Canada), 10 Alcorn Avenue, Toronto, Ontario, Canada M4V 3B2
(a division of Pearson Penguin Canada Inc.)
Penguin Books Ltd, 80 Strand, London WC2R ORL, England
Penguin Ireland, 25 St Stephen's Green, Dublin 2, Ireland
(a division of Penguin Books Ltd)
Penguin Group (Australia), 250 Camberwell Road, Camberwell, Victoria 3124, Australia
(a division of Pearson Australia Group Pty Ltd)
Penguin Books India Pvt Ltd, 11 Community Centre, Panchsheel Park, New Delhi-110 017, India
Penguin Group (NZ), Cnr Airborne and Rosedale Roads, Albany, Auckland 1310, New Zealand
(a division of Pearson New Zealand Ltd)
Penguin Books (South Africa) (Pty) Ltd, 24 Sturdee Avenue, Rosebank, Johannesburg 2196, South Africa
Penguin Books Ltd, Registered Offices: 80 Strand, London WC2R ORL, England

LIBRARY OF CONGRESS CATALOGING-IN-PUBLICATION DATA
McPhail, David, date.
Emma in charge/by David McPhail.—1st ed.
p. cm.
Summary: Emma pretends that she and her dolls spend a day at school.
ISBN 0-525-47411-0
[1. Dolls—Fiction. 2. Play—Fiction.] I. Title.
PZ7.M4788184Em 2005
[E]—dc22   2004021580

Published in the United States by Dutton Children's Books,
a division of Penguin Young Readers Group
345 Hudson Street, New York, New York 10014
www.penguin.com/youngreaders
Designed by Jason Henry
Manufactured in China · First Edition
1 3 5 7 9 10 8 6 4 2

"Time to get up,"

Emma said to her dolls.
"You don't want to be late for school."

But before school came breakfast.

"Eat your banana," said Emma to her redheaded doll.

"Fruit is good for you."

"First we'll add," said Emma.
"How much is one plus one?"

Then she taught the dolls their ABC's.

"Time for coloring," Emma instructed.
"Try to stay inside the lines."

Next came music.

"Sing loud, please," said Emma. "But don't yell."

After that, there was recess.

Then a visit to the doctor for a checkup.

"We're going on a field trip," declared Emma.
"Hold on tight."

"We'll visit the zoo," Emma told the dolls.

"See the Big Cat sleeping?"

Emma saw her mother.

She was planting flowers in the yard.

"Time to go for a ride," said Emma.

"These are yellow flowers, and this is a red one."

Then Emma saw something else.

It was her father.
"Naptime!" cried Emma.

Being in charge had tuckered
Emma right out.